AF075298

# Stage Struck

# Stage Struck

Samantha Montgomerie

Lia Visirin

**Collins**

# Contents

Chapter 1 Stage-struck .................... 7

**BONUS** Learn to speak
    Elizabethan English ..................... 20

Chapter 2 Caught! ......................... 23

**BONUS** Tudor clothing .................... 36

Chapter 3 An unusual request ............. 39

**BONUS** The Globe theatre ................. 52

Chapter 4 A cunning plan .................. 55

**BONUS** A Midsummer Night's
    Dream: characters ...................... 68

Chapter 5 Some sprite-ly magic ........... 71

**BONUS** A Midsummer Night's
    Dream: plot ............................ 84

Chapter 6 A midsummer's dream .......... 89

**BONUS** Elizabethan special effects ........ 104

About the author ......................... 106

About the illustrator ..................... 108

Book chat ................................ 110

# CHAPTER 1
# Stage-struck

The racket of London spilled into the room as Mary opened the shutters. A chamber pot sloshed and splattered as it was emptied onto the street. Horses' hooves clattered on cobblestones. Shouts echoed as street sellers called out to customers.

With sleepy eyes, Mary peered into the early morning sky. The ghostly moon sat suspended as the darkness melted to orange. The fading moon shone with a midsummer magic.

Leaning on the windowsill, Mary imagined herself as an actor on the stage. The words of William Shakespeare would fall on the audience waiting beneath her.

She whispered some of his lines:

"… the morning steals upon the night, Melting the darkness."

The street below was far from her dreamy vision. Mistress Smith was collecting a bundle of laundry for another busy washing day. Master Thorn pulled down his cap as he rushed to meet the ships at the docks. Mistress Green was starting her long walk to the house on the hill to begin her cleaning. No one had time to cast a glance at Mary.

"Mary, make good speed!" called Mother from downstairs. "You will be late!"

Bessie yawned as she lay in their bed beside the window. "Master Shakespeare needs your quick hands to get his sewing done," she said.

Mary lay beside her sister and sighed. "Aye. 'Tis a shame he does not need my talents on the stage," she said.

"Begone with you!" said Bessie. "What good would his plays be without your costumes? They bring his worlds to life."

Mary sighed. It wasn't the same as acting on the stage. It was so unfair that girls were not allowed to perform.

"Mary!" Mother's voice was louder now. It was enough to rouse Bessie to throw back the cover.

"Best we make speed. Master Shakespeare might hear Mother's roar and think she is a lion in his play!" said Bessie.

Mary giggled. She pulled herself out of bed, tied on her apron and made her way downstairs.

"You will earn extra pence if you finish your fairy queen gown today," said Mother.

Mary nodded. She broke a piece of rye bread, taking a bite of its warm goodness. She sighed.

Yesterday, she had worked until the night had cloaked the sky. How her fingers ached! It was only three days before the first night of *A Midsummer Night's Dream* at the Globe.

Mary and the other seamstresses were racing against time to get the costumes ready.

There would be a huge crowd coming to see the play. It was always a favourite. Mary understood why. She loved how it was set across two worlds – the court of Athens and the otherworldly forest just beyond the city's walls.

It made her believe that, with a touch of magic, we could travel to a world of fairies and spells. Mary loved the mischievous fairy Puck. He cast a spell on the human characters and they got in a muddle over who they loved.

Puck's trick on Bottom the weaver always made her laugh. First, he turned Bottom's head into that of an ass. Then he made the beautiful Titania, Queen of the Fairies, fall passionately in love with Bottom!

Titania sent all her fairies to tend to Bottom, while she crooned over his long furry ears. *It showed just how clever Master Shakespeare was*, thought Mary, *making such a tangle with all the characters and then having to untangle them again.*

"Your hard work will bring joy when your costumes go on stage," said Mother. She gave Mary's shoulder a gentle squeeze.

Glancing at the table, Mary could see Mother was getting ready to begin her own sewing. When the morning light got stronger, Mother and Bessie would be pulling their stitches in neat lines to trim the hats which lay waiting. The needles and threads stood to attention, waiting for skilled hands to call them into action.

Mary gave her mother a warm smile. With a flourish, she strode to the door. As dramatically as she could, she recited her favourite lines from the mischievous Puck:

"I go, I go; look how I go,
Swifter than arrow from the Tartar's bow."

Bessie giggled.

"Get you gone!" laughed Mother.

Mary did an elaborate bow, grinning as she gave them a wave. She tied her biggin and headed out into the busy street.

The bustle of the crowd swept Mary along as she weaved her way through the narrow streets. She picked up her heavy wool skirts and kept a sharp eye on the cobblestones, avoiding the stinky contents of a discarded chamber pot.

She wove quickly through the jostling crowds towards London Bridge. She caught a glimpse of the River Thames, its water ruffling in the morning breeze. At least a hundred boats dotted the river. Some drifted with their sails puffed like rounded bellies, tracking a steady path to the other side of the city. Others sliced through the waves, powered by the slick stroke of oars.

Mary threaded through the swarm of people making their way across London Bridge. They streamed from the tall houses. Shop doors swung open. Traders, shoppers, workers and walkers all spilled onto the bridge. Horses and carts clattered through the crowds, their wooden wheels bouncing as they rolled past.

"Ink! Ink! Pen and ink!" The quill seller's voice boomed to be heard above the racket.

"Trinkets and toys! Trinkets and toys!" called the tinker beside him.

Slipping through the people, Mary made her way to the end of the bridge. She trailed down by the Thames, past the towering spires of the church, down to the Globe. Its circular white walls basked in the glow of the summer morning's light.

Mary took quick strides up to the tiring house, where the costumes were made and the actors came to get dressed before a performance.

She could hear the murmur of voices in the yard as the actors began to arrive. But in the tiring house, she was still alone.

Titania's gown lay on the table like a sea of snowy satin. Flowers of the finest silk were sewn with tiny stitches, budding over the fabric.

Hour upon hour, Mary had worked to attach the blooming buds, transforming it into a dress fit for a fairy queen.

Mary looked at the closed door. Should she dare to try the dress on? She lifted it up. Slipping it on over her clothes, she felt the weight of the satin as it draped in flowing folds.

Mary lifted her head high, pulled back her shoulders and held an arm up in a dramatic pose. She imagined standing centre stage with a troupe of fairies by her side.

In her best queenly voice, she recited Titania's lines:

"I'll give thee fairies to attend on thee,
And they shall fetch thee jewels from the deep."

Behind her, the door of the tiring house swung open. Mary stiffened.

An angry voice hissed, "What are you doing?"

# Learn to speak Elizabethan English

aye – yes

nay – no

'tis – it is

thee – you

begone – go away

get you gone – you need to go

come hither – come here

Fie! – Oh no!

Hark now! – Listen!

make haste – hurry

methinks – I think

nought – nothing

time doth fly – time is going quickly

Whither? – Where?

yonder – away; over there

good morrow – good morning

good eve – good evening

How now? – How are you?

fare you well – goodbye

see you on the morrow – see you tomorrow

# CHAPTER 2
# Caught!

In the doorway stood Anne, one of Mary's fellow seamstresses. Mary stared at her with wide eyes. In a flash, Anne turned to shut the door behind her. "Off with that!" she whispered.

Mary's cheeks flushed. Her hands trembled as she tried to fumble her way out of the dress, but she was drowning in folds of satin. Footsteps thumped up the stairs, coupled with the loud voice of Agnes complaining about her sore back. Mary started to panic. She needed to get out of the dress before Agnes arrived!

"Why did you do that?" said Anne. She helped to untangle Mary's arms from the sleeves. "Agnes will throw you out if she sees you!"

Tears stung Mary's eyes. What a careless thing she had done! Her wild dream of being on the stage could now see her ripped away from the very place she loved. Agnes was stern. All the girls knew she would tolerate no nonsense. She had high expectations of her staff.

They were expected to work hard and to stitch well. There was no room for nonsense, let alone for trying on costumes! If Agnes learned of her moment of temptation, Mary knew she would be gone.

Anne pulled the dress over Mary's head just as the door flung open. Agnes towered in the doorway. She scowled at Anne who was clutching the dress in a tangled mess in her arms. The curious face of Jane, another of the seamstresses, peered from behind her.

"Good morrow," said Anne, her voice cheery and bright.

At that moment, Mary admired Anne's ability to put on a good performance.

"Good morrow," said Mary, her voice tight with fear. Avoiding the uncomfortable stare of Agnes's sharp eyes, she smoothed out her ruffled apron.

"We were admiring this needlework," said Anne, fussing over the dress in her arms. "Our Mary has made it fit for a queen of the forest."

Agnes squinted her eyes. Did she know? Mary's stomach tightened.

Agnes bustled inside and scooped up the green silk breeches on the table.

She held out the breeches to Anne. "Time doth fly! Get your thread. Our fairy king also needs his finery," she said.

Mary breathed a sigh of relief. She scooped Titania's dress from Anne's arms, giving her a quick smile to show her thanks. She busied herself with finding her needle and thread, avoiding Jane's questioning eyes.

The sun tracked across the sky, marking the minutes of the passing morning as they stitched. Agnes had pulled back the curtains of the tiring house to let in more light.

The voices of the actors echoed around the empty yard. Over these past weeks, Mary had heard the play so many times that she could now recite all of it in her mind. Bessie called her memory her golden casket – a valuable case that could hold precious things like the beautiful words of Master Shakespeare. But what was the point if Mary could never put those jewels to use?

Jane shuffled in to sit beside Mary and Anne. "Agnes is out yonder. Make haste! Tell me what happened this morn?" she demanded.

"Mary thought she was the fairy queen. I caught her in the dress!" Anne whispered.

Jane sighed. She reached over to squeeze Mary's hand. "Methinks you are masterful at reciting all those lines," she said kindly. "But you must be careful! It will come to nought but trouble."

"Aye," sighed Mary.

"None can stitch as finely as you. Let that be your wonder on the stage!" said Anne.

Anne's words were said with kindness, but they sparked a fire inside Mary. It just wasn't fair. Why were men able to do as they pleased, while women had to sit on the side watching? Why did everyone think a woman's brain was only good for needlework and cooking? Weren't they capable of thinking and acting just as well as any man could?

"Come hither, Anne," said Jane. She placed the shimmering cape of the fairy king on the table. "Methinks we must finish the doublets now."

Anne nodded. She set aside the breeches and followed Jane into the little room at the back of the tiring house.

Mary draped her costume over the stool. She was almost done. She rubbed her tired fingers and stretched. Her eyes travelled to the stage. She could see the actors clearly from here. Henry and Jack were in position as Puck and Oberon, King of the Fairies. The other actors clustered in the yard, practising their lines. Master Shakespeare stood amongst them.

Master Shakespeare clutched a script and watched as the actors took their places. Mary marvelled at this man with his talent for weaving words that moved thousands to tears and laughter. How she wished she could be part of that magic as it unfolded on stage. She knew she could deliver her lines with just as much talent. If only she could be given the chance.

She cast her eyes around the galleries circling the stage. In just three days, they would be filled with thousands of people.

The yard would be swarming with groundlings, pressing against the stage and sprawling into every space. Above the stage, the Lord's boxes would hold the ladies and gentlemen in their finery, facing the audience so everyone could admire them. Mary trailed her eyes to the Heavens, a kind of balcony which jutted out over the stage.

She loved the inky-blue of the sky painted there, and the way the golden sun, moon and stars all shone. With the theatre circling like the globe of the world and the heavens stretching above, Mary felt the joy of this world within the real world. A world where magic and illusion could come alive.

Mary crept to the shadowy edges of the stage and held her breath. Hidden in the dark, she watched.

"Hark now!" called Master Shakespeare to the actors on stage, commanding them to listen. "'Tis time to begin."

Crouching at the corner of the stage, Oberon leaned towards Puck. As he began his lines, Mary's lips began to move.

With hushed whispers, she sounded out each word …

"I know a bank where the wild thyme blows,
Where oxlips and the nodding violet grows.
Quite over-canopied with luscious woodbine,
With sweet musk-roses and with eglantine:
There sleeps Titania sometime of the night,
Lulled in these flowers with dances and delight."

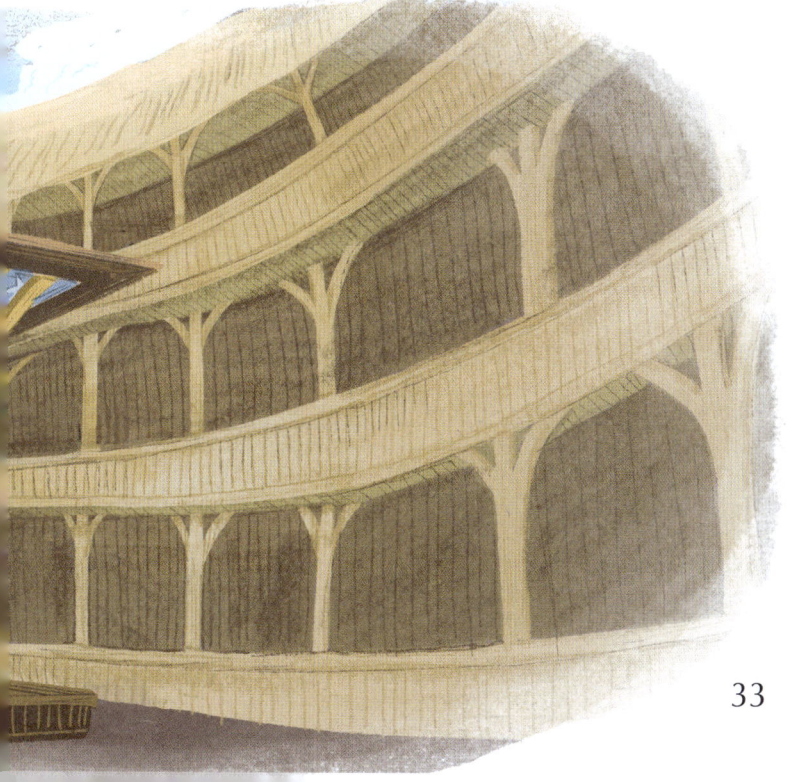

Mary grinned as the words flowed from her tongue. She loved how they sounded. She loved how they felt. Master Shakespeare knew how to make the words roll in your mouth and tingle on your lips. You could almost see the flowers before your eyes.

A rustle in the shadows startled her. A figure emerged. Mary gasped. She covered her mouth to stop more words tumbling out. Before her stood Edward, the actor cast to play Titania.

For the second time that day, Mary had been caught.

# Tudor clothing

Working class clothing in Tudor times.

cap
doublet
pouch
breeches
leggings
buskins

# CHAPTER 3

# An unusual request

"I meant not to startle you," said Edward, as he stepped out of the shadows towards Mary.

Mary was pleased his voice did not hold the bite of anger. Edward was new to The Lord Chamberlain's Men, Master Shakespeare's company of actors. With his handsome features, it was easy to see why he had been cast as Titania. But what if he had heard her saying the lines in the play? What if he told Master Shakespeare that she had left her duties in the tiring house? Mary hurried back to the table, picked up her needle and bent her head low.

Edward followed her into the tiring house. He had just turned 12, the age when boys could take to the stage. With his youth, his make-up and his wig, Mary knew he would make a striking fairy queen. She gave him a slight nod, then cast her eyes back to her work.

In a fluster, Agnes bustled into the room. Her arms were filled with an enormous pair of fairy wings. Small beads had been stitched on the fine silk to look like silvery dew drops.

Agnes stopped when she saw Edward. Mary stiffened. Would he tell?

"Good morrow," he said. "Master Shakespeare sends me for a fitting."

Mary did not dare to meet his eye. Or to look at Agnes. She took her time to knot the final stitch on the gown.

"Aye," said Agnes. "Come hither. Let us fit these now." Edward followed her towards the little room at the back of the tiring house.

As they disappeared from view, Mary sighed with relief. She promised herself that she would keep out of trouble. She just needed to focus on her work. She couldn't afford to lose her job. Each week, it was getting harder for Mother to pay the rent. They wouldn't have food on the table without this money.

Scooping the satin in her hands, she hung Titania's gown on a hook. Hermia's gown was next.

Of all the characters in the play, Hermia was her favourite. *What courage she showed!* thought Mary. She refused to marry a man she did not love, just because her father wanted her to. He even threatened the law of Athens that could sentence her to death for disobeying him. But she didn't care. Instead, she ran away to marry her true love, Lysander. Mary sighed. Such bravery was made only for the stage. How could a woman take such a risk in the real world?

Mary sat on her stool. If she was not allowed to act, she would have to make do with this. Bessie was right. She was still part of the magic, after all. She settled down to work, turning her back to the stage.

Time raced by. Daylight was draining away. The midsummer moon was like a mischievous eye, keeping watch.

"Fare you well," said Jane.

"See you on the morrow," said Anne.

Mary's body ached from sewing all day. She thought of the pottage and bread Bessie would be heating on the stove, and smiled.

As she neared London Bridge, Mary stopped. Edward stood before her.

"Pardon me," he said.

Mary froze.

"I heard you read Oberon's lines," he said.

Hot tears pricked Mary's eyes. "Please. I beg you not to speak of it."

"Nay," said Edward. "You misunderstand me." His cheeks flushed. "What I mean is that I wish for you to teach me."

Mary furrowed her brow. Teach him? Whatever could he mean?

"I am new to the stage. The words don't flow with ease," said Edward. He paused and looked her straight in the eye. "You know all the lines by heart."

Mary's heart leaped. All those weeks of mouthing the lines. Edward had noticed.

Mary looked away uncomfortably. Surely no good could come from this.

"The other men joke when I trip on my lines. I don't like to ask for their help. The words fly from your tongue. You could help me." Edward's eyes searched her face for an answer.

Mary thought of his kindness earlier. If he had told Agnes or Master Shakespeare that she had been reciting lines when she should be sewing, she would be out of her job. Surely she could repay this kindness.

She felt a flicker of something spark deep inside. "Aye," she said. His face broke into a grin. "Come along then." She nodded for him to follow as they joined the bustle of the crowd. "Best we get to work," she said.

As they wove through the crowds on London Bridge, Mary helped Edward with his lines. She imagined they looked like two ordinary friends talking about anything. No one would have guessed she was reciting lines from a play. Besides, that in itself wasn't breaking any laws! Mary's heart soared as she rolled the lines off her tongue, letting herself be first Oberon, then Bottom, as Edward said his lines in return.

As they walked, their footsteps matched the beat of the words. Mary told Edward to take note.

There was a rhythm in the lines. They struck a beat when spoken. This helped to make the words flow.

"If you get stuck, think of the beat. It's as easy as walking," she said.

Edward grinned. "As easy as walking," he replied.

As they reached the other side of the bridge, Edward stopped. "'Tis time to bid you farewell," he said.

Mary thought for a second. What would Mother think if she was to bring Edward home to supper? There was only one way to find out.

"You could join us for supper. We could practise some more," she said.

Edward grinned. "Aye." He cast an eye across the sellers. "Wait here," he said.

He darted to the pieman with his tray of pies held high on his head. Edward dug into the pouch on his belt for his pennies. A meat pie! Mother would be very happy with their supper guest!

The meat pie went down a treat! Mother had warmed to Edward straight away. Bessie had asked him a hundred questions about being an actor in The Lord Chamberlain's Men. He had them laughing over tales of tripping on his long dress and losing his wigs on stage.

Now, in the flickering candlelight, he looked shy.

Bessie started clearing the plates.

"Let us try your lines once more," said Mary.

Mother sat to finish the final stitches on Mistress Smith's hat. "Take no mind of us, lad," said Mother. "This one has been acting since she could talk!"

"Aye! There has been much drama in this house," said Bessie.

Edward grinned at Mary. "Aye. She speaks as well as any man on stage does," he said.

Mary's heart swelled with pride. She stood up and nodded for Edward to do the same.

The midsummer moonlight streamed through the window like a spotlight. Mary stood in the light.

"Let us begin," she said.

# The Globe theatre

**Entry fees**

groundlings – one penny

Lower Gallery – two pence

a cushion – one penny

Lord's boxes – six pence

the Lower Gallery

tiring house

stage exit

groundlings

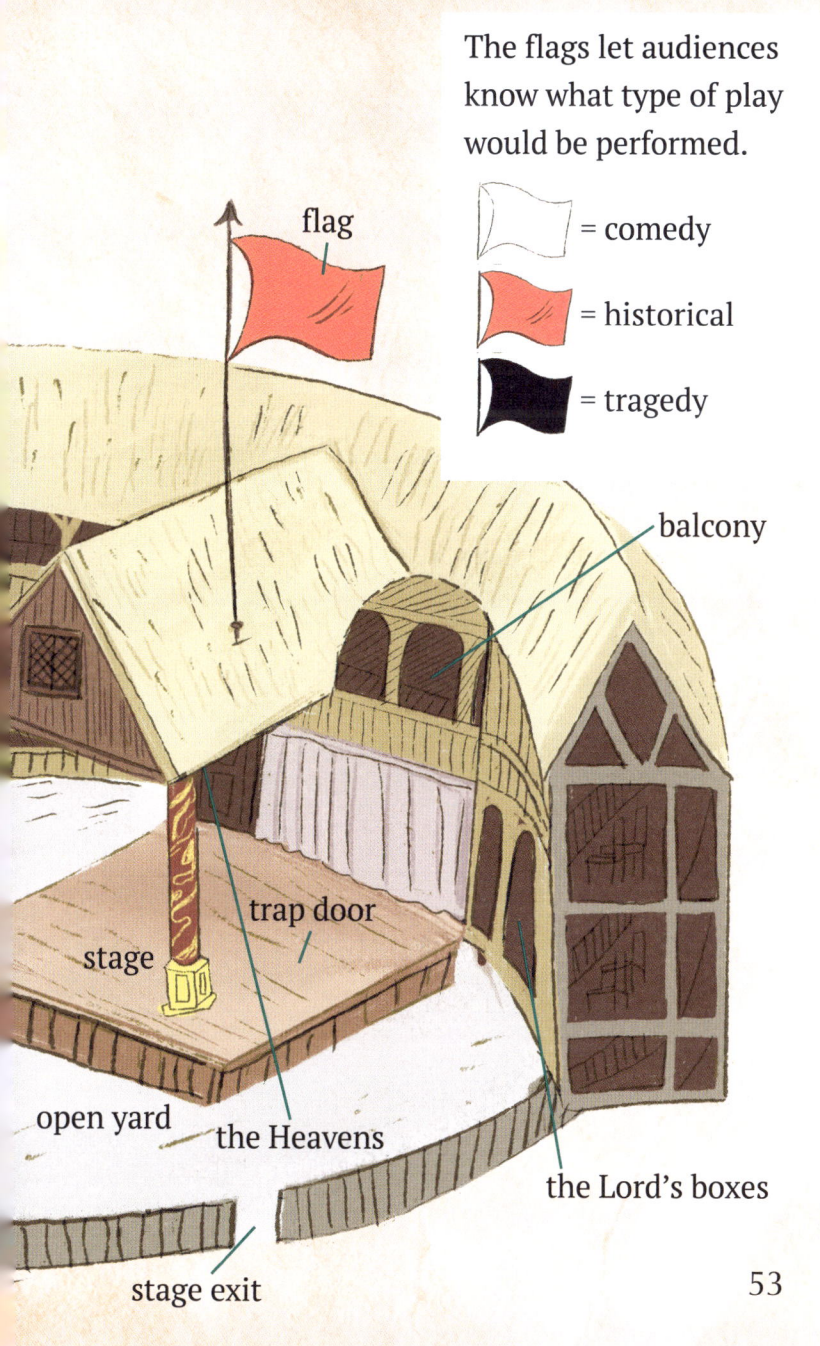

# CHAPTER 4
# A cunning plan

Cobweb's wings needed beading, Lysander's breeches needed tightening and Hermia's cloak needed trimming. It would be another late finish for Mary. She tried to blink the tiredness from her heavy eyelids.

"These doublets need their final stitching, too," said Anne.

"Aye," sighed Jane. She set down the doublet she had been sewing. "There's also the ass head to fix. We must mend his floppy ear before our fairy queen swoons over it." She headed off to find it.

It was the day before the first performance and the theatre was in a whirl. Costumes were piled throughout the tiring house.

Over the last two days, Edward had continued to come back to practise his lines. In the morning, Mary and Edward met as the sun was rising lazily in the sky. They recited the passages as they walked towards the Globe, caught in their own world as the hustle and bustle of London went on around them.

Mary loved their time together! The lines she had memorised were becoming useful. Her golden casket of words was open and she could show off her jewels.

Now, as she stitched, she could hear Edward on the stage. They were practising the scene at the start of the play where Oberon and Titania were fighting over who gets to take care of a young boy. Oberon wants the child for himself. Titania will not give the boy away. He has been put in her care by a dear friend.

This is when Oberon decides to seek revenge by making Titania fall in love with the enchanted Bottom. It was a difficult scene for Edward. Titania has to show her strength. Edward has to convince the audience that she is determined to win this fight.

Mary heard Jack proclaim Oberon's bold command:

"Give me that boy and I will go with thee."

She craned her neck to watch Edward deliver his fiery reply:

"Not for thy fairy kingdom.
Fairies, away!"

His words sounded like steel. They sent shivers down her spine.

"Bravo, Titania!" Master Shakespeare clapped as he praised Edward. "Bravo!"

Mary smiled. Edward was superb!

"He's doing well, that young lad," said Anne. She settled on a stool beside Mary, nestling the enormous ass head in her lap.

"He looked like a spooked hen up there at the start," said Jane.

Anne chuckled. "Aye," she said. "What a magical transformation!"

Mary saw them exchange glances. Could they know? She hadn't told them about how she was helping Edward.

Jane and Anne had warned her that her love of the stage would only come to no good. She didn't want them to make a fuss.

A hacking cough rattled across the yard.

"Are you unwell?" said Master Shakespeare. His words were thick with fear.

The girls craned to see what was unfolding on the stage. Henry was coughing loudly as he tried to speak his lines.

"He's been coughing all morning," said Jack. "He could not even utter a word in the yard just now."

They could see poor Henry bent over as he tried to stop his spluttering.

"Fie!" said Master Shakespeare, as he paced back and forth.

Three of the other actors had become unwell. If Henry was too ill to perform, someone else would have to take Puck's role on stage. But they were losing actors fast!

"Off with you," said Master Shakespeare. He flapped a hand in the air. "Take your rest."

Henry made his way from the stage.

"Let us break," sighed Master Shakespeare. They could see his stress as he strode away.

"Fie. Another one down," sighed Jane.

"Let us hope 'tis not the consumption," said Anne. "That would put us all in our beds!"

"But what will they do?" asked Mary. "What if no replacement can take to the stage in time?"

She sighed. Would all their toil be for nothing?

"It would take someone who knows the lines well," said Anne.

"I don't know if such a lad exists. They've all been struck down with this cough," said Jane.

Out of the corner of her eye, Mary caught a movement in the shadows of the gallery. It was Edward! She scraped back her stool and stood up. "Pardon me," she said.

Hidden in the shadows, she beamed at Edward. "You were most wondrous!" she whispered.

"Thank you," said Edward. "'Tis all because of you." He dropped his voice to a whisper. "Henry is unwell. Master Shakespeare has sent him away! Other boys have taken ill, too."

Mary nodded. "I know. I fear the show will not go on!"

Edward looked her in the eye. "It can. If you wish it to."

Mary furrowed her brow. What did he mean?

"You could be Puck," whispered Edward.

Mary gasped incredulously. "Me? They would never let me! You know women cannot be on the stage."

Edward nodded. "Aye. But what if you were to become a lad?"

Mary stared at him. *Whatever could he mean?* she thought.

"You use costume and make-up to turn me into a woman. Why can't you use the same tricks to turn yourself into a lad?" said Edward.

Mary could not believe what he was saying.

"You know the lines as well as any of the actors. You would make the most wondrous Puck!" said Edward.

"'Tis impossible!" exclaimed Mary.

"Nay!" A voice from behind startled them. Jane and Anne shuffled out of their hiding spot. They had been listening!

"'Tis not impossible," said Jane. "The lad is right. We have been working all hours to turn him into a fairy queen. We can surely turn you into a lad!"

"You have a gift, young Mary. And our Master Shakespeare needs you," said Anne.

Mary couldn't believe what she was hearing. "But what about Agnes?" whispered Mary.

"Don't you worry about her," said Jane.

"We can keep Agnes busy," said Anne.

"First we must convince Master Shakespeare," said Edward. "He is beside himself with worry that he won't find a suitable Puck."

"He was mighty pleased with you on the stage," said Jane. "Methinks he will take your suggestion of a talented lad kindly."

Edward nodded. "When he hears Mary speak, he will be in no doubt."

Mary's head was spinning. Could she really do it? Could she perform on the stage without anyone knowing? She knew Anne and Jane could work their magic to transform her. But could she convince an entire audience? She couldn't bear to think about what would happen to Mother and Bessie if she was caught.

Mary swallowed hard. "But – what if I fail to convince people I am a lad?"

Anne tightened her hand on Mary's arm. "We will make you the most convincing young lad to take to the stage," she said.

"We will not fail," said Jane. "You will be the best Puck that London has ever seen!"

"Come now! Make haste! 'Tis time to perform some magic of our own on Master Shakespeare," said Anne.

# A Midsummer Night's Dream: characters

## The fairy world

Titania – Queen of the Fairies

Oberon – King of the Fairies

Puck – mischievous fairy

The little boy

Peaseblossom, Mustardseed, Cobweb, Moth – Titania's fairies

# The human world

Egeus – Hermia's father

Hermia – loves Lysander

Lysander – loves Hermia

Demetrius – wants to marry Hermia

Helena – loves Demetrius

Bottom – a weaver whose head gets turned into that of an ass

# CHAPTER 5
# Some sprite-ly magic

"Just one more," said Anne, as she did up the last button on Mary's doublet.

"I found the perfect cap!" said Jane. She held the black cap up for Mary to see. "It should hide your lovely locks." She tucked it under her arm as she twisted Mary's plait and pinned it close to her head.

They had leaped into action before Mary could change her mind. Within minutes, they had worked their magic and transformed her. Dressed in a doublet, breeches and leggings, Mary now looked like a young man.

A frantic tapping rattled the door. Mary jumped in fright.

"Agnes comes hither!" called Edward.

Anne put a hand on Mary's arm and gave it a comforting squeeze.

"Fret not. We have our plan," she whispered.

Anne turned on her heel and went out to greet Agnes. Jane put her finger to her lips and raised her eyebrows, signalling for Mary to stay quiet behind the curtain. Mary's stomach twisted with anxiety.

"Agnes, I need help with the ass head. 'Tis troublesome to fix," said Anne.

"Aye," sighed Agnes.

"'Tis out here by the gallery," said Anne.

Mary heard footsteps as Anne led Agnes outside. She sighed with relief. Agnes was out of the way.

Mary's stomach churned. She hoped their plan would work. Jane and Anne were sure they could distract Agnes while Mary spoke to Master Shakespeare. If Master Shakespeare let her take to the stage, they would tell Agnes that Mary had come down with the cough. They all knew that would work.

Agnes was afraid of the consumption. She would want Mary far from the tiring house if she were unwell. Jane would then send a messenger boy for Bessie to help with the final stitching of the costumes in Mary's place. All it took now was for Mary to convince Master Shakespeare that she was a young lad who could bring Puck to life on the stage. It would be the most extraordinary act of her life.

Jane fitted the hat over Mary's head, tucking up the loose strands of hair. She cast her eye over Mary and grinned. "Perfect!" she whispered. "Now, get you gone!"

Mary slipped out as fast as she could from the tiring house and down the stairs. How free it felt to stride in breeches!

Edward was waiting for her. His face broke into a wide grin. "Good eve, young lad," he said.

"Let's make haste," said Mary, "before I change my mind!"

Master Shakespeare was pacing in the yard with his shoulders stooped and his brow furrowed.

Edward whispered in Mary's ear. "Hark. Remember, do not get too close! Keep to the stage," he said. Mary nodded. "Now go! Show him what you can do!"

Mary strode up the stairs at the side of the stage and paused in the shadows. Taking a deep breath, she stepped out.

"Pardon, Master Shakespeare. Can I speak with you?" Edward said.

William Shakespeare turned to face him. "Edward!" he said. He placed a hand on his shoulder. "Wondrous performance, my lad." Jane was right. Shakespeare was pleased with Edward due to his performance. Perhaps he would listen to him.

"Make haste," said Shakespeare. "I must find a lad to play Puck or our toil will be for nought."

Edward cleared his throat. "Methinks I can help, Sir," he said.

He gestured towards the stage. "Behold. My friend Tom would make a most excellent Puck."

Shakespeare turned his head, noticing Mary for the first time. Mary felt the full weight of his gaze. She hoped he did not notice her quivering legs. She pulled her shoulders back and smiled confidently. Edward was right. She *would* make an excellent Puck. And this was her opportunity to show it.

"Master Shakespeare, 'tis an honour," said Mary. Her voice was as deep as she could get it to avoid raising suspicion.

Shakespeare sighed. He waved his hand dismissively. "'Tis too late to teach a new lad the lines," he said.

"Aye, but Tom knows the script by heart," said Edward.

Shakespeare raised his eyebrows. He eyed Mary again. "Does he? How?" he enquired.

"Allow me to show you," Mary said, and took a bow.

Shakespeare gave a slow nod. He took a few steps to stand facing the centre of the stage. "Aye, then. Begin!" he said. He rolled his hand in the air, signalling for her to start.

Mary's heart leaped in her chest. Which scene should she do? There had been no time to think! It had to be one that showed Puck's mischief. It had to be one that showed him revelling in his tricks. It had to be one where she could bring his sprightly magic alive. Mary knew just the scene.

She would introduce herself to Master Shakespeare on stage in the very scene where the mischievous Puck meets the audience for the first time. In the scene, Puck tells a wandering fairy some of his tricks. He recalls how he pretends to neigh like a horse, and to bob like a crab in a woman's bowl before she goes to drink. It was filled with his mischief. It was filled with fun. It would let Mary bring Puck's magic alive!

Mary stood still on the stage. She looked Shakespeare straight in the eye. She began her lines:

"I am that merry wanderer of the night.
I jest to Oberon and make him smile – "

She grinned mischievously, puffing out her chest at her boastful lines.

"When I a fat and bean-fed horse beguile,
Neighing in likeness of a filly foal."

Mary threw back her head and neighed like a horse, laughing as she galloped and turned across the stage, just as Puck would.

"And sometimes lurk I in a gossip's bowl
In very likeness of a roasted crab,
And when she drinks, against her lips I bob."

Now, Mary had crouched down low, bobbing like a crab with its pincers held high. She clicked them playfully. Her voice was lively, capturing Puck's playful words.

With a dramatic twirl, she turned to the exit at the back of the stage. She pointed towards the entrance where Oberon would stride in. She dropped her voice to a whisper.

"But look, fairy. Here comes Oberon!"

Putting a finger to her lips, she eyed her audience, crouching down. She fixed her stare off into the distance, as if waiting for the King of Fairies to arrive. She was quiet and still.

Silence. Mary's heart hammered so hard she wondered if everyone could hear it. It felt like time was standing still.

Applause broke the silence.

"Bravo!" called Shakespeare. He threw back his head and laughed. "Bravo!"

Mary's heart leaped. He liked it!

Shakespeare patted Edward on the back. "Thank you, lad," he said.

He turned to Mary. "Now, let us make haste, Tom! We have a play to get ready."

# A Midsummer Night's Dream: plot

Hermia ❤ Lysander. Her father wants her to marry Demetrius.

Hermia and Lysander run away to the woods. Demetrius follows them. Helena ❤ Demetrius. She follows him.

In the woods, Oberon and Titania fight over a young boy.

Oberon sends Puck to get a special flower to cast a spell on Titania. It will make a person fall in love with the first thing they see.

Oberon hears Demetrius telling Helena to leave him alone.

Oberon tells Puck to put a spell on Demetrius to make him love Helena.

continued ➡

Puck puts a spell on Lysander by mistake! He falls in love with Helena.

Oberon casts his spell on Titania.

Puck sees Bottom in the woods and turns his head into an ass.

Titania wakes and falls in love with Bottom.

Oberon puts a spell on Demetrius. Now they both love Helena! This makes Hermia cross.

Oberon sees the mistake and makes Puck put things right.

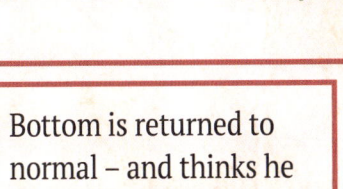

Bottom is returned to normal – and thinks he has had a dream.

Hermia and Lysander, and Demetrius and Helena all get married.

Order is restored in the fairy world. Puck and the fairies bless the humans on their wedding night.

# CHAPTER 6

# A midsummer's dream

The trumpet called across the city, announcing it was time for the play to begin. On top of the Globe, a white flag flapped, signalling a comedy was about to be performed. The crowds swarmed to the theatre.

Within the tiring house, Mary looked as if she had stepped out of a fairy world. Her silky green breeches and doublet were covered in fabric leaves, as if made from the forest itself.

Willow branches had been twisted into bracelets and hung at her wrists. Above her boots, her leggings snaked with green ribbons, twisting like vines up her legs.

"Agnes thinks this new lad is a marvel on the stage," giggled Anne.

Mary smiled. Even the steely-eyed Agnes could not see through her disguise! At least, not yet. Mary felt the knot in her stomach tighten. She still had to convince the audience.

Bessie had taken Mary's place making final adjustments to the costumes, just as they had planned. Mary was happy she was there.

"Ready yourself, Mary!" said Bessie. She lifted the headdress and placed it on Mary's head. It was a spectacular wreath of flowers, leaves and berries, with two antlers placed at the top. With her hair pinned underneath, the wreath would hide it perfectly. Wearing a fake beard and green face paste, Mary felt well disguised.

"You are the most wondrous Puck!" said Bessie.

"You are a wonder!" said Anne.

"Show them all that you are as good as any man!" said Bessie.

"Now, make haste! The play needs its star!" said Jane. "Best we tend to the others,"

From the edges of the stage, Mary watched the crowds spill into the theatre.

Groundlings filled the yard, jostling and elbowing their way to the front. The smell of roasted hazelnuts wafted on the air as sellers displayed their fruits, nuts and gingerbread.

The galleries were filled with people taking their seats. Some were dressed in their fine gowns, sitting upright and making a show of being seen in their bright silks and high ruffs. The noise was incredible!

Mary's legs quivered. What if her performance wasn't good enough? She knew the crowd would boo or yell if they didn't like an actor on stage. Some of them even threw food!

Edward joined Mary to stand at the side. "You look magnificent!" he said.

Mary beamed at him. His face was covered in a fine white paste to give his skin a complexion that sparkled like the stars. The powdered bones and poppy oil made the perfect mix. He had added red blusher from the ground root of the cinnabar to his cheeks and lips, giving him a rosy glow.

A dusting of crushed pearls created a shimmer on his skin. Coupled with his long brown wig, his crown, his flowery gown and his beaded wings, he made a radiant fairy queen.

"We will be magically magnificent!" said Mary. Edward had worked so hard. She knew he was ready. She repeated the words in her head, trying to convince herself that she was ready, too.

The trumpet blared, long and loud. It was time for the play to begin.

The audience loved the opening act. The story had been set. They cheered as the fierce Hermia told her father she would not marry Demetrius, and instead plotted to run away to marry her true love, Lysander. They laughed at poor Helena as she pouted, moaning and groaning, wallowing in self-pity that she was not beautiful enough for Demetrius.

They had shouted out joyfully as boastful Bottom claimed he could play every single part in the workmen's play. The key characters had charmed the audience, who now waited to see what would happen to them all in the mystical forest. It was time for the fairies to appear.

White smoke furled around the edges of the stage. The lilting of a flute and the strings of a lute suggested a magical mischief was in the air. A small fairy wandered out. That was Mary's cue.

From the opposite end, she scampered onto the stage, an impish skip in her step. She playfully cast her eye out across the audience. A cheer erupted from the crowd. Mary's heart soared! With a sprightly spring in her step, she scuttled over to the wandering fairy. Parading as Puck, she delivered her opening line:

"How now, spirit! Whither wander you?"

Mary felt alive! Of course she had felt the joy of reciting Shakespeare's lines at home. But here, she felt the thrill of hearing the crowds cheer as she spun her magic before them.

Now, crouching beside Oberon at the edge of the stage, she showed them how much the mischievous Puck enjoyed watching Titania under the spell. The fairy queen swooned over Bottom with his ass head cradled in her hands.

Edward peered adoringly at the ass and gestured for his fairies. In a lovesick voice, he told them to:

"… pluck the wings from painted butterflies,
To fan the moonbeams from his
    sleeping eyes."

The audience erupted in laughter. Edward was superb!

What magic it was to spin their tale on stage! Mary felt sad when the play came closer to the end. She loved how the audience cried and cheered as their happy ending was delivered. Hermia was allowed to marry Lysander, Demetrius declared his love for Helena, and the King and Queen of the fairies found peace with each other again. The final lines, however, belonged to Puck.

For the first time, Mary fully understood the weight of these final words. Puck asks the audience to think about just how much of what they had seen on the stage was real. Mary had herself been part of a magical illusion. Not just in her role of Puck, but in pretending to be a boy. In this world within the world, she had been able to perform. She had been not herself but also her true self.

Mary cast an eye to Bessie, beaming from outside the tiring house. Things had to change. With all her heart, she hoped they would, so Bessie and every young girl could be seen as equal to any man.

Taking centre stage, Mary delivered her closing lines:

"If we shadows have offended,
Think but this and all is mended:
That you have but slumbered here
While these visions did appear.
And this weak and idle theme,
No more yielding but a dream."

Cheers erupted. Applause rumbled like thunder. Calls of "Bravo!" echoed throughout the theatre. Mary's heart was singing.

"Well played, lad," called Master Shakespeare from the wings.

The other actors flooded onto the stage. Edward slipped his hand into Mary's and raised it high before pulling them down into a dramatic bow.

The paper-thin shadow of the midsummer moon hung in the afternoon sky. Mary grinned up at it, silently thanking it for sending her this midsummer's dream.

# Elizabethan special effects

## Storms

- Firecrackers sparking up a wire to the Heavens looked like lightning bolts on stage.
- Cannonballs rolled across the floor or the beating of drums created thunder.

## Battles

- Cannons fired gunpowder in battle scenes.
- Animal bladders filled with animal blood made stage blood.

# Ghosts

- A trap door allowed characters to emerge from the 'grave' or 'from hell'.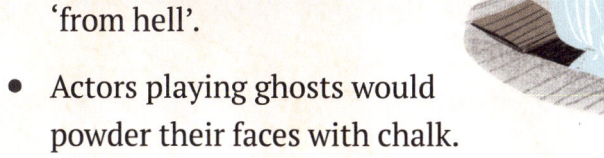

- Actors playing ghosts would powder their faces with chalk.

- Good spirits entered from a trapdoor in the Heavens.

# Magic

- Metal wires called 'flies' allowed actors to fly across the stage.

- White, red, green and black smoke was made from mixing chemicals together.

- Music was used with live musicians to add magical sound effects.

# About the author

**Do you prefer writing fiction or non-fiction?**

There is a lot of fun to be had with both types of writing. When writing fiction, you can create new worlds, unusual characters and make just about anything happen! Writing non-fiction is also really interesting – there are so many fantastic things to research and I love exploring new topics. *Stage Struck* allowed me to combine these two things.

**Samantha Montgomerie**

A historical novel means you have to do a lot of research and then think of an engaging story to bring that time period to life.

**How do you go about writing a book like this?**

Writing a historical novel always starts with researching the time period you're setting your story in. When I decided to write a story in the Tudor period, I knew I wanted to set it at the Globe theatre as I have always loved Shakespeare's plays. I read lots of books and articles online which told me what London was like during this time, and what it was like for actors and seamstresses working at the Globe. When writing, it was important to keep checking that the details were correct – what were women's skirts made of at the time? Where did people empty their chamber pots? What did they use for make-up when making male actors look like women on the stage?

**What's your favourite thing about writing?**
Bringing characters to life! It's such a pleasure to think of a character like Mary and write a story which makes her seem like a real person. It sometimes takes a long time to get this right. My characters often sit in my head for a while, telling me what they think and feel. Sometimes I'm surprised at what they do when I'm writing the story. I didn't know Mary was going to try on Titania's dress in the tiring house – but when she did, it made perfect sense!

**Why did you want to write this book?**
Reading stories about people who overcome obstacles is always inspiring. I wanted to write a story with a character determined to be their true self, without anyone holding them back. The setting of the Globe proved the perfect 'stage' to let this story unfold.

**What do you hope readers will get from the book?**
A love of Shakespeare's comedies! Mistaken identities, mischievous fairies, magic and mayhem – what is there not to love? I really hope they will watch *A Midsummer Night's Dream*, as his plays were made to be performed. I also hope that Mary and Edward show them how important being a good friend is. With supportive people by our side, we can do anything!

**What do you hope happens next in the story?**
I hope that Mary and Edward get to perform together again at the Globe. And that maybe Agnes gets to stumble into the mystical forest to meet the mischievous Puck for some more midsummer magic! I wonder what Puck would turn Agnes into?

# About the illustrator

**How did you get
into illustration?**

I've always loved drawing, especially stories. As a child, I'd fill notebooks with sketches of characters and scenes. It wasn't until much later that I realised illustration could be my profession. I started studying children's books and practising different styles, and from there, I built a portfolio and started working with authors and publishers.

**Lia Visirin**

**What was the most challenging thing about illustrating this book?**

The most challenging part was finding the balance between historical accuracy and emotion. Tudor times had a very specific look – costumes, buildings, even how people lived. But I also needed the characters, especially Mary, to feel relatable and full of life. So it took some experimenting to get that mix right.

**What was your favourite scene to illustrate?**

Definitely the moment Mary steps on stage as Puck. It was so fun to draw her costume.

**Have you seen any Shakespeare plays?**

I've seen a few, including *A Midsummer Night's Dream*, which has always been one of my favourites.

**Do you do lots of research for historical scenes?**
Yes, research is a big part of the process. For this book, I studied Tudor clothing, tools used by seamstresses, the layout of the Globe theatre, and how people lived day to day in that time.

**Which character do you identify with the most?**
I think I relate most to Mary. That feeling of having a creative spark but not always the freedom or confidence to show it – that's something I've felt too. Like Mary, I've had people in my life who encouraged me to take a leap, and it made all the difference.

**Which character was the most fun to draw?**
Edward! He has this supportive, playful energy. Plus, drawing Titania's costume on him was a highlight.

**Have you ever acted on stage?**
Only in school plays – and I was always nervous! But I do love the theatre, and I think that helped me imagine what it might feel like to be behind the curtain, heart racing, waiting to step into the spotlight.

**How did you come up with designs for the costumes in the play?**
I looked at existing sketches from old Shakespeare plays and studied what materials and colours were common at the time. Then I added some extra touches to show the personality of each character. For Titania, for example, I made sure the dress felt fairy-like and flowy, with lots of delicate flower details.

# Book chat

Had you heard of William Shakespeare or the Globe theatre?

Have you ever seen a play?

How do the characters help Mary to realise her dream of performing?

What do you hope happens next in the story?

Why do you think Shakespeare is still famous today?

If you could ask any character from the book a question, what would it be?

Which part of the story did you find most exciting, and why?

Who do you think was the bravest character in the story?

Which character do you think changes most from the start of the story to the end?

How do you think Mary's life is different from your life today?

## Book challenge:

Design your own costume for a sprite or fairy.

Published by Collins
An imprint of HarperCollins*Publishers*

The News Building
1 London Bridge Street
London
SE1 9GF
UK

Macken House
39/40 Mayor Street Upper
Dublin 1
D01 C9W8
Ireland

© HarperCollins*Publishers* Limited 2025

10 9 8 7 6 5 4 3 2 1

ISBN 978-0-00-876795-2

All rights reserved. No part of this publication may be reproduced, stored in a retrieval system, or transmitted in any form by any means, electronic, mechanical, photocopying, recording or otherwise, without the prior written permission of the Publisher or a licence permitting restricted copying in the United Kingdom issued by the Copyright Licensing Agency Ltd, 5th Floor, Shackleton House, 4 Battle Bridge Lane, London SE1 2HX.

Without limiting the exclusive rights of any author, contributor or the publisher of this publication, any unauthorised use of this publication to train generative artificial intelligence (AI) technologies is expressly prohibited. HarperCollins also exercise their rights under Article 4(3) of the Digital Single Market Directive 2019/790 and expressly reserve this publication from the text and data mining exception.

British Library Cataloguing-in-Publication Data
A catalogue record for this publication is available from the British Library.

Download the teaching notes and word cards to accompany this book at:
http://littlewandle.org.uk/signupfluency/

Get the latest Collins Big Cat news at
collins.co.uk/collinsbigcat

Author: Samantha Montgomerie
Illustrator: Lia Visirin (Advocate Art)
Publisher: Laura White
Commissioning editor and
    product manager: Caroline Green
Series editor: Charlotte Raby
Development editor: Catherine Baker
Project manager: Emily Hooton
Copyeditor: Sally Byford
Proofreader: Catherine Dakin
Cover designer: Sarah Finan
Typesetter: 2Hoots Publishing Services Ltd
Production controller: Katharine Willard

Printed in the UK.

 **MIX**
Paper | Supporting
responsible forestry
FSC™ C007454

This book contains FSC™ certified paper and other controlled sources to ensure responsible forest management.

For more information visit: www.harpercollins.co.uk/green

Made with responsibly sourced paper and vegetable ink

Scan to see how we are reducing our environmental impact.